AF436794

STRUCTURAL INTEGRITY

TABITHA O'CONNELL

STRUCTURAL INTEGRITY

CONTENT NOTE

This book contains depictions of:

- Sexual situations (non-explicit)
- Disordered eating
- Alcohol consumption
- Classism
- Anxiety

I

Now

Kel lay on his stomach before the open balcony door, a cool night breeze tickling his skin. The brown-striped cat that sometimes managed to climb up stared at him from the stone balustrade. After a moment, it dropped to the floor, still watching, and Kel stretched his arm toward it. "Come on, don't you want to explore in here?" The cat stood still, one paw lifted, large pupils glinting back the room's dim gaslight.

Hunger tugged at Kel's stomach, and he drew in a long breath and embraced the feeling, lowering his head to let his cheek rest on the rug. He hadn't eaten since breakfast, save a plum off one of the courtyard's trees.

Behind him the room's door clicked open, and the cat darted away into the darkness. "What are you doing?" came Yaan's bemused voice. The lights brightened, and Kel rolled onto his back and stood, measuring his speed so his head wouldn't spin.

"Nothing. How are you?"

"Exhausted. Today was the longest day." Yaan fell onto the bed and reached out a hand toward Kel.

Kel stepped forward to clasp it. "Sorry." Perching beside him, he smoothed Yaan's hair back above his closed eyes.

"Mmm." Yaan pressed into his touch, shifting to nuzzle his face against Kel's palm, his stubble tickling slightly. "My only comfort was knowing I'd be coming back to you."

Kel's hand slid to the fastenings at Yaan's throat. "You had an important meeting today, right?" he asked as he worked the first set free and moved down to the next. Removing Yaan's administrative robes was always a process. "How did it go?"

"Oh, it was fine. Not worth talking about." Yaan's eyes blinked open and focused on Kel's. "Help me forget it?"

The lightheadedness brought on by the lack of

nutrients in Kel's body was akin to tipsiness, making him lazily compliant. After reaching an adequate state of forgetfulness, Yaan snuggled against his side and fell asleep. Kel lay still for a bit, but his empty stomach won the fight against his drowsiness. Eventually he eased away and crept off to steal dinner from the kitchens.

Then

The first time they'd met, when Kel had breached Yaan's office door after finding the outer desk clerk absent, Yaan had spent a long moment staring at him before shaking his head. "Sorry. I wasn't expecting—um. I mean. Hi."

"Hi." Kel smiled and stepped forward to hand off the note that bore Yaan's name, the satchel at his side full of others bound for different officials and departments. "I've got this for you."

Yaan rose to take it, eyes intent on Kel's face. "Thank you. I haven't seen you here before."

Kel shrugged. "Well, you have now." He gave Yaan a grin before turning to go.

"Wait..." Looking back, Kel caught Yaan's face tinging pink. "Sorry. Just—what's your name?"

"Kel."

"I'm Yaan. ...Which you probably already knew."

Yaan's eyes dropped, but Kel lingered. In the course of his job he'd had people make remarks to him, including propositions, but no one had ever seemed *flustered* by his presence before. Much less someone with at least several years on his nineteen, and a government position to boot. He found himself mildly charmed by it.

"Yaan," Kel repeated, and Yaan's eyes darted up again. "It's nice to put a face to the name. Hopefully I'll see you again."

"You could stop by next time you're here." Yaan sank back into his chair, smoothing his robe. "I mean, even if you don't have anything for me. If you'd like."

"Sure, all right."

That night Kel spun his family the story of the government official who was infatuated with him, but thought little else of it—until the next time his job brought him to the Complex, when he did, indeed, go back.

Now

"You're up early." Yaan's arms slid loosely around Kel's shoulders from behind, the silk of his dressing gown sleeve tickling Kel's throat. Kel welcomed the warmth. From his spot at the balcony railing, he'd been playing a game with a child across the courtyard, exchanging exaggerated mimes and gestures. The child was waving frantically now, pointing at him because it was his turn, but he mouthed *Sorry*, and the kid slunk inside.

"Can I come with you today?" Kel twisted until Yaan's profile came into view. Yaan wasn't pretty; he appeared older than his years, with a nose that some would say was too large, hollows beneath his eyes, and a mouth that tended to turn down at the corners. But Kel hadn't yet gotten tired of studying him.

"What, to the office?"

"Where else?"

"But why would you want to come there?"

"Enthil is sick so I've got no harp lesson today, they haven't gotten any new books at the library, and Master Thom kicked me out of the pigeon roost."

A puff of breath hit Kel's neck. "Should I ask why

you got kicked out, or why you were there in the first place?"

"I told you, I love the pigeons! They're beautiful and sweet."

"...Pigeons."

"But Thom said I was getting in the way and just because I used to be a delivery boy didn't mean I had a right to hang around the roost."

"Well, he's right."

"I just don't know what to do with myself now. So I want to come with you, and keep you company. Like before."

"You know I go to my office to work." Yaan said it lightly, giving him a quick squeeze.

"You had work then."

"Yes, but *then* that was my only chance to see you. Now I get to see you here, every day."

Kel hesitated a moment before replying. "All right."

"Maybe another time. When I'm less busy." Yaan bent his head to kiss Kel's neck. Across the courtyard, the kid was back, and miming gagging.

"Come keep me company while I get ready?" Yaan asked, and Kel followed him inside and chattered more about the pigeons while Yaan washed, shaved, and muttered to himself over a missing sock. On his way out the door he pulled Kel to him and whispered in his ear, "I'll see you tonight."

"One of them I named Zara," Kel said to the empty room. "She just looked like a Zara somehow." He'd said the same thing to Thom, and suddenly he could see why the man might've been inclined to shoo him away. Heaving a sigh, he knelt to look under the bed for his boots.

Then

Kel had soon made a habit of visiting Yaan every time he was at the Complex. "So, what do you do for your job, exactly?" he asked once, and Yaan sighed, and said it was too dull to bother describing.

"You tell me about your job. How long have you been a delivery boy?" The word "boy" lit a warm glow inside Kel's chest, and he gladly told the tale of his career.

While he could have stayed all day entertaining Yaan, he had work to get back to, so they agreed that Yaan could ask him one question each visit. The queries ranged from "Tell me about your family," to "Tell me a funny story," to "Tell me your favorite thing." Once, Yaan greeted him with, "Only one earring today?", which Kel insisted counted as his question after relating how he'd lost the other. The next time he came, Yaan presented him with a small box containing two perfect golden hoops.

Yaan continued to avoid talking directly about himself, but Kel teased out a picture of him—prone to worry, miserable at social functions, committed to his work but also exhausted by it. It seemed a rather sad life, and Kel loved being able to bring him some small measure of joy. Eventually, he started to imagine other ways he might do so.

"You're here." On one visit, Yaan rose from his chair and strode to meet Kel, grasping his hands. "I've been having the worst day. I'm so glad it's you."

It was the first time they had stood so close; the first time they had touched. Kel smiled and left his hands in Yaan's grip. Yaan glanced down at them, then back up at Kel. Kel squeezed ever so slightly.

"Tell me..." Yaan leaned in, voice dropping low. "Do you want to come to bed with me?"

Warmth spread over Kel's face; this was leaps beyond what he'd expected. But Yaan's willingness to ask thrilled him. He looked down, biting his lip while he recovered from the surprise, trying to hold back a ridiculous grin. Finally, he breathed, "Yes."

"Now?" Yaan's thumbs rubbed over the backs of his hands.

"I... have messages..." He made himself say the words, but the obligation seemed suddenly petty in light of Yaan's offer.

"We can sort that out later." One of Yaan's hands slipped free and lifted to caress Kel's cheek. "I'll take responsibility if you get in trouble. I'll make up for any pay you're docked."

Kel let his smile break free. "All right."

Now

Kel slipped into his family's house and followed the sound of arguing voices to the kitchen. He'd been glad it was a free day for his two sisters, meaning he'd get to see them as well as Sarrin, but perhaps that wasn't ideal after all.

For a moment he hung back in the doorway. Beni, always the responsible sibling, was on her knees picking dried beans off the floor, while Trayna faced off with their parent over her head.

"I told you to be more careful!" Exasperation dripped from Sarrin's words.

"I *was* careful!" Trayna countered.

"Hi," Kel said, and they all looked at him.

"Oh, hi Kel," Trayna muttered, already turning back to Sarrin. Beni looked up and smiled at him as Sarrin stepped over the spilled beans to give him a quick hug.

"We'd concluded that official wasn't ever going to let you come back and see us," she said, pulling away to study him.

"Oh, no, it isn't his fault. It's me, I've been lazy."

"You look thin. Is he not feeding you?"

"No, he feeds me too much!" As soon as he said it he glanced back at the beans that Beni had returned to painstakingly rescuing one by one, and was struck by a pang of guilt. Yaan had given him two notes now, money for his family to cover his lost salary. Both still rested in a corner of the drawer where he'd tucked them away. He knew what Sarrin and Vari, his other parent, would say if he tried to make them take it.

"Hmm." Sarrin eyed him for another long moment, and to distract her—and help Beni—he dropped to his knees and began scooping up beans. With a sigh, Trayna knelt by his side, while Sarrin asked, "Why doesn't one of you get the broom? It would be much quicker."

"We're almost done," Beni answered, and Sarrin sighed and shrugged and turned back to the half-chopped vegetables on the counter.

Then

Yaan had told the clerk he'd been called away on important business, and then strode through the hallways as if it were true, head high with purpose and dignity, Kel trailing after. A locked door on the second floor led to the residential portion of the Complex, where the carpet was thicker, the halls dimmer and quieter. It felt like any moment someone was going to pop out of a doorway and demand to know what Kel was doing there.

Yaan sighed when he closed the door of his room behind them. His eyes met Kel's, and he smiled—it always completely changed his face, the tension melting away. Then his hands were on Kel's shoulders, easing him back against the wall, running down his arms to pick at the knot of his sash.

"Wait—" As the fabric loosened around his waist,

Kel grasped Yaan's wrists, stilling his hands. Yaan's eyes jumped to his, body drawing back slightly. Kel gave him a smile of reassurance and let go to tug his shirt over his head, leaving himself standing before Yaan in his chest wrap. "I just need…" He gestured at the pins holding it in place.

"Oh. Here." Yaan stepped behind him, cheek brushing against Kel's hair, arms reaching around to pull the pins free. Kel's breath caught in his throat—the warmth of Yaan's chest against his back, the sweetness of Yaan helping him…

"Just loosen it a bit," he said softly, and Yaan complied, pinning the fabric less-constrictively back in place. His hands dropped to circle Kel's now-bare waist, sending his skin tingling, and his mouth met Kel's neck, trailing down to trace his collarbone. Heat bloomed in Kel's cheeks. He tilted his head back to brush his lips against Yaan's face, then twisted in Yaan's arms to finally kiss him, fingers weaving into Yaan's thick hair. This was the moment he'd been seeing in his daydreams.

Yaan's teeth grasped at his lips momentarily, his hands clutching Kel closer, before his mouth slid aside to rove over Kel's jaw and down his neck again. When he lifted his head, face flushed, he paused to gaze at Kel.

"You're so beautiful." He shook his head slowly, as if in disbelief, and then grabbed Kel's hand and drew him toward the bed. When they reached it, Yaan flung himself onto the mattress and looked up at Kel. "Take my clothes off?"

Kel did his best, laughing as the robes sought to thwart his efforts. Yaan helped him, and said, offhand, "You'll learn." Kel raised an eyebrow at that and grinned.

With the layers of robes a crumpled bundle on the floor, Yaan settled against the pillows. Kel knelt over him to kiss down the soft, pale skin of his chest and stomach.

Eventually, Yaan gasped out, "Wait," and dropped a hand onto Kel's shoulder. "What about you?"

Kel lifted his head just long enough to smile at Yaan. "You first."

Now

It was nice being with his family. Eventually Vari got home, and was happy to see him, and didn't think he looked any thinner. When Yaan came up, though, she radiated disapproval.

Kel ate supper with them all, at Sarrin's urging, but then she and Trayna got into another fight, and Beni disappeared into her room, and Kel told Vari he was going to go. She glanced in the direction of the bickering and nodded, rolling her eyes. "I wonder why. But look, Kel, if you ever want to come back and stay... you know you're welcome to, right?"

"I do." He smiled at her and leaned in to kiss her on the cheek. "But I'm fine there. Yaan treats me well. You don't need to worry."

"All right..." She didn't sound convinced.

"Kel's leaving?" Sarrin called from the kitchen, appearing a moment later with Trayna behind her. After hugs all around, Kel stepped out the door.

The sun had dipped low, casting the streets in golden light, and the neighborhood was quiet. He tried to shed the odd discomfort he felt, imagining it sloughing off him to be left behind on the ground. As he walked he took in the worn familiarity of the Second Ward— streets lined with frame two-family houses, some with third stories cobbled on and staircases hastily constructed against the side walls, lines of drying clothing stretching across the alleys. Two cats darted by, and a chicken pecked at the cobblestones.

Kel turned onto High Street, where the facades of the shops lining either side boasted large windows and bright-colored doors. A block further down, impressive as ever, rose the old Second theater.

This building had been three stories from the beginning, and Kel had been told that on show nights a row of lanterns would be hung from the cornice. The entire ward would gather there, the older residents said, some even coming up from the First, to socialize as much as to watch the show. The theater sold the best spiced wine in the city, and the performers weren't half-bad either.

All Kel's life, though, the building had sat empty, looking faded next to its more vibrant neighbors, its windows boarded like closed eyes. They'd lost their liquor license on some technicality, and profits dwindled away until the owners could no longer afford to sustain it.

Kel stopped when he reached the building, admiring the way the sun struck its stone facade. He'd always wanted to go inside, to see for himself the place that was etched so fondly in the previous generations' memories, but he'd never been daring enough to break in.

"Still beautiful after all these years, isn't it?" A man

with a face collapsed into wrinkles stepped up next to him, craning his neck for a better view. Kel opened his mouth to agree, but the man went on, "A shame it's coming down soon."

"What?"

"Yep, saw it in today's paper. They say it's a safety hazard and needs to go." The man shook his head. "I was at the very last show, you know. They held it for free—no need to charge when the place was closing, eh? Everyone came out for one last good time together. Back then it felt like we were all family. Now what're we supposed to do, hike up to the Third and pay those prices? Those appointed bastards don't want us gathering and being friendly. They want us fighting each other so we won't recognize they're our real enemies."

He eyed Kel then, perhaps noticing the cut of his garments for the first time. It was his plainest set of clothing, but with a second look it was easy to notice the quality of the cloth, the fine stitching. Yaan had insisted on buying them for him. "Say, you're Vari's boy, aren't you? The one who caught the eye of one of them up at the Complex and lives there now?"

"Yes..." Kel looked at his boots for a moment before

rallying. "But I love the theater too! I didn't know they were tearing it down. I'll talk to him and see if there's anything he can do..."

The man turned his back and started walking away, flapping a dismissive hand. "Oh, sure, you'll talk to them, and feel like you've done your part, and then you'll forget about it. You're one of them now."

"No..." Kel watched him go and then looked back at the building. It appeared strong as ever. Why was it suddenly a safety risk now?

Words he'd grown accustomed to seeing scrawled across messages rose in his mind: *Yaan Travers, Property Dept.* On impulse he walked up and touched the sun-warmed stone, fingertips brushing a promise across its miniature crevices. Then he turned away and made for the Complex.

Then

Afterward, Yaan had held Kel tight against his chest. "I'm not letting you leave," he mumbled into the back of Kel's neck.

"I'm already late," Kel answered regretfully, tracing one of Yaan's fingers with his own.

Yaan lifted his head. "I'll take care of that; it won't be a problem. But I didn't just mean now. You could live here. With me."

"Oh." Kel eased out of Yaan's grasp and rolled over to face him, trying to read whether he was serious. There were no signs that he wasn't.

"Now that I've got you in my bed, I can't bear the thought of my bed without you in it." Yaan smirked and rested his hand on Kel's hip. Kel's lips curved into a slight smile as his eyes darted away.

"And I suppose I could keep my job..."

"You could, but there would be no reason for it. I'll see to it that you have everything you need."

"My family, though... I mean, most of the money's for them."

"Then I'll see to it that they have what they need, too."

"I..." Kel looked at Yaan, a cloud blotting out the brightness in his chest. "I'm not looking to be... kept," he said at last, softly.

Yaan's eyebrows jumped. "Oh—that's not what I meant at all. I'm trying to say, of course I'll take care of you and your family, if you're to be my lover."

The words were a wind, whisking the cloud away. A smile broke over Kel's face, and he pulled Yaan close to kiss him.

Now

"Kel." As Kel stepped into the room, Yaan was rising to his feet, setting down a glass of wine, walking toward him. "Where were you?"

"I went to see my family." Kel stopped, frowning at Yaan's anxious expression. "But never mind that, I just heard they're tearing down the old Second theater!"

Yaan pressed a hand to his eyes. "Kel, you can't just disappear like that."

"What do you mean? I 'disappear' every day."

"But you're always here when I get back." Yaan sank down on the couch again, lifting the glass for a long drink. "You're always here."

"I'm sorry, I didn't mean to worry you. I just... wasn't thinking."

"Is that supposed to comfort me?"

"But, Yaan, the theater—they can't tear it down. Everyone loves it, it meant so much to people, and it's not in bad shape, it could be reopened someday..."

Yaan waved his arm, motioning Kel over, and Kel came and sat beside him, and let Yaan drape his arms around him, pulling him close and speaking into his hair. "It's sat empty for, what, over two decades now? If no one's reopened it yet, they're not going to." Kel twisted and pulled away slightly to face Yaan, but Yaan went on, "I know it's a nice building, but the city's got other theaters."

With a sigh, Kel turned his head away. "It's not the same."

"Kel..." One of Yaan's hands rose to stroke his hair. "We can talk about this more, but can it wait for now? I've had a long day, and then I sat here worrying something had happened to you..."

Kel looked back at Yaan—at the dark circles under his eyes, the stubble on his cheeks that always made him look haggard. He lay a hand on one of those cheeks, and dragged his mouth into a smile. "Sure, yeah. Sorry I worried you."

Then

For Kel's first Complex party, Yaan had gotten him a set of dress robes, and helped him put them on, and told him he looked ravishing and that he wished they could just stay in for the night. Kel found the robes heavy and cumbersome, but he forgot them momentarily when he stepped into the great hall. He'd peeked into the room before, but now the two chandeliers were lit, casting a glow upon the tables of food lining the periphery and the scatterings of couches and low tables occupying the rest of the space. In one corner his harp teacher played strains that drifted over the government officials and their companions, who sat or stood about, proud and prim and impeccably dressed.

Yaan paused in the doorway, but Kel grabbed his hand and drew him in, looking around in wonder. "Kel, look ou—" Yaan tugged him to a stop, and he turned to find he'd almost run into someone.

"Oh, sorry."

"Quite all right." The man was taller than either of them, and had another man on his arm, shorter yet equally imposing. "Evening, Travers," he went on. His eyes flicked to Kel. "This must be the boy we've been hearing about."

Yaan drew himself up taller. "Yes, this is Kel. Kel, this is Ubay Wrin, Deputy Commissioner, and Irandan Psay, head of the sewage department."

"Pleased to meet you." Kel felt like he should bow, but knew that would be silly. The impulse remained anyway.

"He is just as pretty as I heard," Psay commented.

"And you've got him all dressed up, how charming," Wrin added.

"Yes, well, if you'll excuse us, we're off to get something to eat." Yaan gave the pair a quick nod, then turned away and drew Kel after him. "I was selected for my position over Psay," he murmured close to Kel's ear. "He hasn't let go of his grudge."

The next person Yaan introduced him to barely nodded at Kel, and then she and Yaan got to talking about some government business. Soon, tired of trying to eat with his plate balanced in one hand, he slipped away to find somewhere to sit.

A woman sipping a drink alone on a couch nearby made eye contact with him and waved, and he waved back uncertainly with the hand holding his fork. She smiled. "Kel, is it?" He smiled back and sat down in the chair next to her.

"That's right. How did you know?"

"I'm sure most everyone knows by now. You're the talk of the party—Travers's pretty new boy."

"Oh." She had to be exaggerating; he hadn't noticed anyone paying him particular attention.

They chatted about the food and the clothing until her eyes slid beyond him and she said, "He's coming to steal you back. But, listen..." And she tilted her head close to Kel's. "If he ever starts to bore you, come visit me, hmm?" She winked just as Yaan walked up.

"I think she's married to someone in the tax department," Yaan said as Kel accompanied him away. "What did she say to you?"

"Oh, nothing, just empty party talk."

He didn't have any interest in the woman's offer, nor any worry about Yaan's reaction. But when he thought about repeating her words, his skin prickled with shame.

Now

Kel bid Yaan goodbye from bed the next morning, only getting up after Yaan's departure. He wanted to find out more about the impending demolition of the theater, but where did he even start?

Bathed and dressed, he stopped by the dining room and grabbed a pear, and, on a whim, traced the path down to the kitchens. In the doorway of the main room he paused, eyes scanning the array of moving figures. After a moment he slipped in among them, returning smiles and greetings, and made his way to the far side. There, in the massive larder, he found her: Jennibel Landers, head cook, known to everyone as Lannie.

"I can't believe we're out of cinnamon," she was saying to a girl who stood beside her looking helpless. "Well, we're just going to have to get creative."

"Hi."

Lannie turned at Kel's greeting, her lips quirking briefly. "Hey, Kel. How are you keeping?"

"Fine. I wanted to ask you about something?"

"Well, it'll have to wait for now." She spread her hands, indicating the cinnamon situation and the general pandemonium outside the larder.

"That's all right. Can I help with anything?"

Stepping up to a shelf, Lannie reached into a basket and drew out a large piece of ginger root that resembled a giant, asymmetrical insect. "Here." She pressed it into the girl's hands and then pulled out another for Kel. "Peel and chop."

It felt good to be useful. Kel stood between the girl and another boy he knew and chatted with them while they all worked. Soon after his arrival he'd been exploring the Complex and stumbled upon the kitchens, where Lannie had asked if he needed anything. He'd introduced himself and found out she'd grown up in the Second Ward and knew Sarrin, and from then on the kitchen had been somewhere he could go when he wanted company while Yaan worked. A few of the staff had made jabs at him at first, sharp with resentment, but now the perpetrators mostly ignored him, and the others didn't seem to mind his presence.

He was juggling bits of ginger while his two companions lounged against the counter and egged him on when Lannie called, "Hey, Kel, come join me and let those two finish their job." With a sheepish look at his audience, he caught the chunks and slunk away to where Lannie stood in the larder doorway.

"I'm redoing the inventory myself, because somebody obviously wasn't paying attention last time," she explained, eyeing the ledger in her hand and then squinting at the shelf in front of her. "Here, write down what I tell you. Starting with five pints of honey." Kel hastened to adjust his grip on the book and scrawl down the words. "Six quarts of molasses. Now, what did you want to ask me about?"

"Have you heard they're tearing down the Second

theater?"

"Are they? That's a shame." She paused to glance at him. "When we were kids, I would always sit in the balcony with Sar and some other school friends, and we'd try to sneak some of the wine. Two and three-quarter bags of sugar."

"I tried to ask Yaan about it, but—he didn't really listen." Kel scribbled down *Sugar, 2.75.* "I know he's head of the property department, but what does that mean, exactly?"

Lannie sighed as she shifted a large sack aside. "Well, it means that if the theater is being torn down, he'll probably have been directly involved in the decision. Six and one-half bags of flour."

Kel swept his toe through some spilled yellow powder on the floor, drawing a curved line. "He didn't mention that last night."

"Eight pounds of salt. Are you going to try bringing it up again? The least he could do is explain the reasoning behind it."

"Yeah, it's worth a shot, I guess." Kel straightened and smudged the line out.

"Two crates of apples."

"Oh, um..." Kel's eyes returned to the ledger, where

he'd only written two entries. "I think I missed a few?"

Lannie held out her hands, and his face warmed as he returned the book and pencil to her. "It's all right," Lannie told him, "you've got other things on your mind." She gave his shoulder a quick pat. "Best of luck with the talk."

"Thanks." He smiled at her before stepping out. Weaving through the gauntlet of kitchen workers, he paused to reach for a piece of flatbread from a basket and almost crashed into a boy carrying a load of firewood. As he ducked out of the way, apologizing, the boy cast him a dirty look and muttered, "Watch it, whore."

Then

Yaan had come in upset one evening, grumbling half-sentences, shucking off his outer robe and letting it fall to the floor. He sank down on the couch next to Kel, and while Kel hadn't been able to parse what was wrong, that didn't matter. He rubbed a hand across Yaan's back, and Yaan let out a long sigh, shoulders relaxing a bit. After some moments of silence, Kel's fingers moved to Yaan's face, cupping his cheek. Yaan looked up at him, and even as exhausted and defeated as he seemed, his mouth quirked slightly upward. Kel smiled himself, and then leaned forward to bring their lips together.

He kept it light and soft, and when Yaan shifted and grabbed Kel's bottom lip in his teeth, Kel slipped free and kissed across Yaan's cheek, up to his ear, before moving back to his mouth. Again Yaan pushed harder, his tongue probing against Kel's teeth, but Kel broke the kiss, brushed his lips across Yaan's again for just a moment, and sat back.

"What?" Yaan asked, forehead slightly wrinkled as he regarded Kel.

Kel laughed slightly and looked down at his hands, now resting in his lap. "I wanted to relax you, not wind you up." Really, what he'd pictured was his show of affection melting Yaan's bad mood away, so that they could loll together on the couch while Yaan filled him in on what had happened. And then they would kiss some more before getting in bed, just to sleep, Kel holding Yaan while he drifted off.

"Mmm, but I like it when you wind me up." Yaan stretched, sat up straighter, and slid a hand onto Kel's thigh.

"But what about your bad day?" Kel twitched his

hand to bump lightly against Yaan's. "Don't you want to talk about it?"

"Ha, no, it's better forgotten."

Yaan's hand squeezed, and Kel leaned toward him again. He and Yaan just had different ideas of what was comforting, apparently. Yaan looked at his lips, and traced them with one finger before rising to strip off his second layer.

Now

When Yaan came in, Kel was lying on the bed, staring up at the ceiling. Earlier he'd managed to coax the cat into the apartment, letting her sniff around on cautious feet, but he'd put her out again before long. Yaan wouldn't want animal hairs on his robes.

"Kel?" came Yaan's voice as the door closed. Then, with relief: "There you are." He walked up and rested a hand on Kel's foot. "What are you doing?"

"Waiting for you." Kel put on a smile, but otherwise didn't move. "How was your day?"

"No worse than usual." Yaan's fingertips ran over the sole of Kel's foot, making him twitch, before sliding up his leg.

Kel pushed himself up with one hand and grabbed Yaan's collar with the other, pulling him down, and Yaan smiled and kissed him quickly before scrambling onto the bed, rolling over Kel to lie beside him and pull him close. Kel had no energy—he'd ended up feeding his stolen flatbread to a dog and hadn't eaten anything in its stead—but he didn't need it. Barely feeling Yaan's mouth on his neck, he asked softly, "Was it your decision to tear down the theater?"

"Hmm?" Yaan stilled and drew back, frowning slightly. "Why would you think that?"

"Because that's your job." Kel's voice stayed quiet. "Isn't it?"

"Such things do, ah, fall under my purview, yes."

"Why didn't you mention that last night?"

"I..." Yaan paused, taking a long breath, then went on more softly, "I didn't want to upset you."

"So it *was* your decision." Kel searched Yaan's face, and Yaan's eyes slid away.

"Not exactly. I didn't set out to tear the place down. We were approached by someone interested in buying the property, and when the building was assessed, it was found to be unsafe. So it's got to go."

"It can't be repaired?"

"Maybe it could, but the buyer isn't interested in that. They're going to take it down once the sale is finalized."

"But you don't have to sell it. You can wait, and see if someone else wants to fix it up."

"There's no sense in turning down a perfectly good offer. Do you know how long the building's sat empty? We're lucky to have anyone interested in that parcel at all."

Kel stared at Yaan, out of rebuttals but not remotely satisfied. "I just wish you'd told me," he finally said, eyes dropping to the coverlet between them.

"I'm sorry." Yaan's hands tightened on his back. "I should have. Forgive me?"

Kel met Yaan's eyes again and answered by pushing himself up to bring his lips to Yaan's, letting them linger, both a lie and a question. At first Yaan kissed him back, gently and sweetly—but then his hand lowered to slip beneath Kel's loose tunic. Drawing back, Kel caught it by the wrist and forced a smile. "You first."

It was easy to brush away Yaan's subsequent offer to reciprocate. "If you're sure," Yaan answered, squeezing Kel's hand where it rested on his stomach. "Have a bath with me, then?"

Kel shifted, reclaiming his arm and drawing his knees up to his chest. "I'm tired—I think I'm just going to go to sleep."

"Oh. All right." Yaan was still for a moment, then kissed his cheek and got up, apparently without having noticed the tears pooling in Kel's eyes.

Then

On one of Yaan's rare free days they'd dragged the couch onto the balcony, and Kel had stretched across it with his head in Yaan's lap. One of Yaan's hands ran lazily through Kel's hair, the other holding a glass of wine. Kel still hadn't developed a taste for the stuff, even though Yaan said he would if he drank it more often. It seemed like too much work with too little payoff.

Kel had his eyes closed against the sun's brightness. Children's shouts came from the courtyard below, along with parents' scoldings. Yaan's fingers brushed his scalp, trailed to the ends of his hair, and disappeared momentarily before repeating the action. Kel felt as content as he'd ever been.

"Have you had other lovers?" he asked, tone lazily curious. He hadn't particularly thought about it before, but now he wondered if Yaan had spent moments like this with other people. Yaan had never given any hint either way.

Yaan's hand stilled. After a moment, he answered, "One." His fingers found the gold hoop in Kel's ear and turned it from side to side.

"What happened to them?" Kel asked softly, eyes opening as he shifted to tilt his face up toward Yaan's.

"He left." Yaan paused to take a long drink of wine. "He was offered an appointment in Genden, and he took it."

"Oh." Kel had so many more questions—what had he been like, had he and Yaan argued over the new appointment, had Yaan thought of going with him... Did Yaan miss him?

But Yaan wasn't a prattler like he was, and Kel wasn't about to try to make him one. He let his eyes fall shut again, re-settling his head on Yaan's thigh.

"It was a good thing in the end." Yaan's voice brightened, and his fingers resumed their prior occupation. "Otherwise I wouldn't have you."

Kel's face stretched into a smile, and his hand lifted to rest on Yaan's knee.

Now

Kel feigned sleep when Yaan got back into bed, but it took him ages to actually doze off. When he finally did, it was only to awake again before dawn and lie there until the morning bell chimed and Yaan stirred beside him.

"I told you I didn't want to be kept." Kel's voice came out cracked.

"What?" Yaan shifted toward him, squinting. Kel cleared his throat.

"I told you at the start—but look at me now. You've put me up here so you can..." Kel let the sentence go, let Yaan's mind fill in the rest.

"Kel, what are you talking about? Where is this coming from?"

Yaan sounded genuinely incredulous, but that wasn't exactly reassuring. "I don't mean anything to you." Kel stared off into the room, speaking the words dry-eyed and without emotion; it was easy to do after thinking them all night. "I'm just a body."

"Kel." Yaan gripped his shoulder, startling him with the suddenness and fierceness of the gesture. "That's not true."

"Isn't it? You want me in your bed, and otherwise, I'm just a nuisance."

Yaan's fingers squeezed tighter. "*No.*" His voice was stripped bare; gone was the nonchalance he so often put on, gone was the manufactured confidence. The word was raw and rough with emotion. Kel turned toward him, hope budding in his chest.

"Kel—I could never—" Yaan paused for a moment, and gave his head a shake. "Of course you're not. I've just been under so much stress lately—I didn't mean to neglect you, I didn't mean to make you think..."

A heaviness remained clamped around Kel's heart. "The theater..."

"Yes—do you want to talk about it more? I can show you the reports, I can explain it further, whatever you want."

"Now?"

"Well, no, not immediately, I have meetings, but come by my office around noon?" Yaan's widened eyes held his, face expectant, concerned.

After a long moment, Kel breathed out and relaxed his tensed limbs. "Sure. I'll come then."

"Good." Yaan's lips curved toward a smile, but as he

pushed himself up, he looked down at Kel and hesitated. Kel looked back at him, not sure what he wanted. Finally Yaan just let out a slight laugh, and brushed a hand over Kel's hair, and left the bed.

Then

It was odd having nothing to do. Yaan was paying for harp lessons, but there was something ridiculous about it—what use was there in him, Kellian Insporo, knowing how to play the harp? While exploring was still appealing, he'd learned his way around the Complex already, and learned that most of its occupants didn't like to see someone wandering about aimlessly. The kitchens were always busy; he couldn't spend all day there getting in the way. The whole of the city was at his disposal, but up here in the Fourth Ward he was so far away from the lively bustle of the docks, too far for it to feel worth walking there and back. And it would be silly to go hang around his family's house every day now that he'd moved out. Especially when most days, most of them wouldn't be home.

He went to his harp lessons, because Yaan had already paid for them and because it was something to do. He got to know the pigeons; he hung around the Complex's outer courtyard, chatting with the freelance messengers. One day he went to the Second Ward market just to see all the wares and people, and thought about buying something for Yaan, but then realized that was silly—Yaan didn't need any cheap trinkets. Besides, he didn't have any money with him. He hadn't needed to buy anything since he'd moved to the Complex.

No money meant no market food, even though the sizzle of frying dumplings called to him from a nearby stall. By the time he got back the hunger had faded, and the skipped meal left his memory until, when Yaan returned, a wave of dizziness hit him as he stirred from his sprawl on the couch.

Yaan didn't give him a chance to go snatch something to eat, so Kel just let himself feel the hunger, the fuzzy sort of weakness it brought on, the way it continued to make his head spin slightly. When he focused on it in that way, it almost felt good.

Now

"Kel." Ori, the desk clerk, raised an eyebrow at him as he walked into the outer office a few minutes before noon.

"Haven't seen you for a while. What brings you back here?"

Ori had never been as friendly or as brusque as some of the other clerks, leaving Kel uncertain where they stood. "I'm here to see Yaan."

"Mm, sorry, he's in a meeting." Ori looked at him expectantly.

"Oh, well, I'll just... wait then." Kel took a seat on the long cushioned bench behind him. Ori nodded and went back to his papers.

Kel tried not to stare at the ornate clock that stood against one wall. Other people came in and out of other offices; some looked at him and their faces betrayed recognition, but only a few actually acknowledged him. He smiled at them and murmured greetings, his eyes always sliding back to the clock.

"You know," Ori said to him during a lull in the traffic, shortly after half-past the hour, "I can just let him know you came by."

"I have an appointment with him." Kel lifted his chin. "He was supposed to see me at noon."

Ori's mouth twitched. "Well, I'm sorry, but he didn't say anything about that to me. But surely you can reschedule?"

Heat was creeping into Kel's face. He had a sudden, foreign urge to shout at Ori, but he swallowed and just said, "I'll wait a bit longer." Ori shrugged and ignored him again.

When the clock chimed one, interrupting Kel's cataloging of the rug's pattern, he stood abruptly. Ori's head lifted. "I'll tell him you came by."

Kel didn't answer, but simply turned and walked out of the room. And kept walking, through the corridors, across the outer courtyard, and out the Complex gate.

II

"Thank you, Commissioner. Good day," Yaan repeated, holding his office door open for her, and she farewelled him and departed. He hung back as if he weren't going to follow, but once she'd left the outer office he stepped up to Ori's desk. Kel's absence glared as brightly as a flame.

"Was Kel here?"

"He was, yeah." Ori lifted one shoulder in an indifferent shrug. "Waited an hour, then left."

Yaan turned on his heel. Long strides carried him to the door of his room, which he opened with a tense hand. "Kel?"

No answer—no Kel. All right, so he'd gone somewhere else. Yaan forced his breathing slow and even. Maybe he would come back to the office later. Maybe they would talk tonight instead.

When he returned, Ori said, "Short meeting, eh?"

Yaan passed him without stopping. "If he comes back, let me know, all right?"

Then

One afternoon during his first week at the Complex, Yaan had been busy with paperwork, hand already cramping from clutching the pen too tightly, when a pair of elbows thumped onto his desk. "Excuse me, clerk?"

Yaan had seen the man who now loomed over him around the office before, but he hadn't taken any notice of Yaan until now. Another man lurked in his wake; both wore the deep green robes of officials.

"Hi—I mean, good day. Can I help you with something?"

"Oh, we just wanted to welcome you." An insincere smiled accompanied the statement. "I'm Ubay Wrin, Head of Assessment. And you're... Yann, was it?"

"Yaan. Yaan Travers."

"Yaan." Wrin tasted the name as if it were a mealy

fruit. "Fresh out of university, hmm? Where are you from?"

"Caldeff," Yaan answered, naming the smaller port town to the north.

"Ah—did you go to the academy there?"

"I didn't receive formal schooling as a child, actually." Yaan managed to keep his voice even and maintain eye contact. He knew where this would lead.

The second man snorted, while Wrin sent his eyebrows toward his hairline. "Ah. I suppose you were educated in your parents' warehouse, then, or some similar establishment?"

The flavor of disdain was subtle, but Yaan's palate had learned to discern it well during his university years. Knowing what he would face, his parents hadn't tolerated any laziness or error, hammering into him that he only way he might succeed among people like these was to be beyond reproach.

"Yes," he confirmed. Somehow he was able to sound downright placid. "It provided me with valuable experience."

Wrin smirked at him and abruptly drew away. As he left with his friend, he tossed over his shoulder, "I wouldn't be quite so confident of that."

Now

As Yaan's fingers gripped his doorknob that evening, he already knew Kel wasn't inside. Heavy silence emanated from within, and no light spilled out beneath the door. Still, his eyes scanned the room as soon as he turned up the gas. Nothing had been disturbed—Kel's slippers stood neatly in the corner, as they had since a servant had straightened them; the low table by the couch was empty of books or food; the coverlet lay untouched.

He stood with a hand still pressed against the door, heart accelerating, fear crawling in at the edges of his mind. *Breathe.* He closed his eyes and listened to the voice in his head, until he was able to lower his stiff arm to his side. Kel had come back late just the other night. He probably hadn't been planning to be gone this long. Yaan could just imagine him having dozed off somewhere—in a corner of the kitchens, on the floor of the pigeon roost, by the fire at his family's house. He would wake, see what time it was, and hurry back, and then they would talk about everything. Knowing Kel, he would even apologize for worrying Yaan.

The quiet was smothering him. He opened the balcony door to let in some noise, and then he opened the wine cupboard.

Then

On annual-review day, Yaan had waited with his chest clenched tight, underarms prickling with sweat. He'd been head of the property department for nearly a year now, and hadn't committed any major blunders. But sometime in the next few hours the commissioner would be stopping by to study him with her unreadable face and tell him any and every way he'd disappointed her.

A light tap on the door made him jump, even though he'd been anticipating it all day. Ori poked his head in. "Messenger boy's here to see you."

Relief bloomed from the boulder in Yaan's chest. Kel had actually heeded his request to return. "Excellent. Send him in."

A moment later, there was Kel, that vision of dark-eyed beauty, full to the brim with boyish, unselfconscious charm, projecting carefree ease—some of which seemed to rub off on Yaan just from being in his presence.

"Hi," Kel said, mouth curving into a genuine smile as the door shut behind him.

"Hi." Yaan wanted to just stare at him, but made himself go on. "This is a pleasant surprise. I was expecting the commissioner. Come sit?"

He gestured to the chair opposite him, and Kel stepped forward to perch on its edge. "Just for a minute, I'll have to get back to work…"

"Of course, of course. So." At that word, Kel's eyes ceased wandering around the office to rest on him. "Tell me about yourself."

"Um, well, I live with my family in the Second Ward; I've got two older siblings but they're off on their own, so it's just me and my parents and the younger two at home now."

Yaan nodded, and Kel started to say something else, but another knock sounded against the door.

"Yes?"

Ori leaned in, his gaze catching on Kel before he announced, "Commissioner's here for your review, but she'll do someone else first if you're not free."

"Sorry, yes, as you can see I'm still tied up." Yaan pointed his chin at Kel, who had started to rise but now sat back down.

"Right. I'll let her know."

When the door closed again, Yaan found Kel giving him a questioning half-smile. "You don't want to see the commissioner?"

"Not on annual-review day." Yaan's mouth twisted wryly. "I don't suppose you could stay the whole afternoon?"

"No... but I could go find you some rancid meat or something." Kel grinned. "I'm sure getting sick would also do the trick."

He was so lighthearted—had he ever worried about anything in his life? Admiration overshadowed Yaan's envy. "As disgusting as that sounds, right now I would almost consider it."

Now Kel's smile was sympathetic. "Sorry. I'm sure it will go well, though! I mean, I don't know anything, but I'm sure you're good at your job."

Gods, and he was sweet, too. Something stirred in Yaan, something that felt oddly like sadness, although he couldn't imagine why.

"That's very kind." He forced the words to come out at a normal volume, even though they wanted to be murmured. His eyes, though, refused to rise from his desk.

He drew in a breath, let it out, and looked up at Kel with a smirk on his face. "I just hope the commissioner agrees."

Now

Yaan drank himself to sleep on the couch. At some point in the night he woke, one arm numb from serving as a pillow, and stumbled to the bed, his bleary mind assuring him he'd wake in the morning with Kel beside him.

He didn't. And when he didn't, panic took over. He threw on his dressing gown and went straight to the dining room, asking the vaguely familiar faces if they'd seen Kel that morning or last night. None had.

He tried the pigeon roost next, but Thom hadn't seen him either; nor had Enthil, nor Lannie down in the kitchens... And he was getting curious looks and raised eyebrows for running around in his dressing gown. He retreated to his room and got properly dressed and shaved, then walked mechanically to the office. What else could he do? Kel was gone.

Then

After a particularly harrowing meeting, during which the commissioner had bluntly brushed aside his suggestion to allocate some funds toward fireproofing the housing in the First Ward, all Yaan had wanted was to see Kel. Sometimes he half-feared Kel would no longer be there when he got back. He'd been cold for so long that now, with the thick, soft blanket of happiness draped over him, he couldn't stop touching it to make sure it was real.

When he opened the door, Kel's bright smile welcomed him. "Hi." Yaan smiled back and dropped onto the couch by Kel's side, bending to tug off his shoes.

One of Kel's bare toes brushed his arm. "You look exhausted. Bad day?"

Yaan kicked the shoes away and flopped back. "Yeah, it was shit. Thank the gods it's over now." As he spoke, Kel scrambled up and hopped over the couch, and a moment later his fingers were pressing into Yaan's tight shoulders. "Mmm. What about you, what did you do today?"

"Well, first…"

Partway through, Yaan realized he wasn't taking in Kel's words; he couldn't banish the echoes of the meeting from his mind. He should've read the commissioner's mood better, should've waited to talk to her alone instead of in front of Wrin and the two other department heads… But Kel's hands were easing the tension in his back, and when they moved up to the bare skin of his neck, Yaan twisted to brush his lips over Kel's fingertips.

Kel went still, and Yaan craned his neck to look at him. "What is it?"

"Oh, just… that was odd timing, is all."

"Sorry." Yaan winced. "I may have missed the last thing you said…"

"It was just that Marda's baby's sick. She should be fine, though."

"Right. Sorry, I'm just so tired…"

"It's all right." Kel slid his hands down, beginning to pluck at the fastenings of Yaan's robe.

Yaan helped him, and breathed a long sigh as Kel slid the fabric from his shoulders. Finally, his mind was shutting up.

Now

Poring over deeds to trace the title to an heirless estate wasn't proving a sufficient distraction. Yaan's eyes scanned the same pages over and over; he found he'd forgotten to add a date to his list. When he set down his pen for a brief break, intending to massage his temples, his hand instead reached for his top desk drawer. He drew it open, and his fingers crawled to the back and felt around until they brushed fine metal.

At first, Kel had tried to refuse Yaan's gift of earrings—"You shouldn't have, really, I already replaced the lost one"—but Yaan had insisted until Kel eased his old hoops free and slid the new ones into their place. When Kel had departed that day, the old had remained behind on Yaan's desk.

Yaan withdrew the tiny rings from the drawer, tracing the curve of one with his finger. They were only brass, slightly different sizes, a bit tarnished and bent. They belonged in the incinerator, but he'd always meant to offer them back to Kel. Or at least, he'd told himself that was why he'd kept them, looped together and stashed away.

He pinched the metal tight between his fingers, then stared down at the curved imprint in his flesh, watching it fade. Kel had left—just walked away, without a note or a word. Yaan wanted to believe it was only temporary, that if he were just patient, Kel would reappear at his door. He wanted to believe it hadn't been his fault about the meeting. How could he have known the commissioner would come by for an hour-long chat about other stagnant properties they might be able to sell?

The problem was, if his meeting had been with anyone but Kel, he would have told the commissioner he had a prior engagement. When had Kel become the lowest rung on his ladder of priorities?

Shit. The least he could do was give Kel an apology. If Kel wanted nothing more to do with him afterward, so be it. But he owed Kel that.

Then

"Excited for the party?" Yaan had asked Kel on the eve of the event as they strolled through the inner courtyard. It would be Kel's second one, but Kel had barely mentioned it, which filled Yaan with vague unease.

"Oh... I was thinking, um, that I actually wouldn't go?" Kel glanced at Yaan, unmasked uncertainty on his twilit face.

"Oh? Why not?" Yaan's facade of nonchalance remained firmly in place.

With a shrug, Kel looked down, kicking a pebble off the path. "I just feel like I don't belong there. I don't have anything to say to those people, you're all talking business... And I don't know how you wear those robes every day. They're so heavy!"

Yaan's lips twitched in a brief smile, but his mind was running over the last party, searching for moments that would have made Kel feel out of place. Wrin's condescending sneer as he and Psay had talked about Kel as if he were Yaan's pet. The bare minimum of acknowledgment he'd received from some of the others. The lascivious look on the face of that bored woman. Of course he didn't want to go back.

But without him there Yaan would be alone again, facing the snobbish crowd with no one at his side. Having Kel along meant he had someone to talk to in the moments when everyone else was already wrapped up in conversation. And it showed them all that there was someone who enjoyed his company. When Peyan had left, he hadn't been sure he'd be able to go to a party alone again; he had, but it had been as unpleasant as expected. He'd thought, now that he had Kel, that he wouldn't need to repeat the experience.

Forcing a light tone, Yaan asked, "Well, what should I tell everyone when they ask where you are?"

"They won't ask about me. Will they?"

"Of course they will." Yaan stopped, turning to face Kel and grabbing his hand. "They'll say, 'Where's that absolutely gorgeous young man of yours, Yaan? He looked so fetching in his robes last time, we were all just waiting to see him again.'"

Kel laughed a little as his eyes darted away. "Tell them I tripped on the robes and fell and bruised my face."

"They won't believe you could ever be so clumsy."

"Tell them I'm wasting away with consumption—they'll like that, won't they?"

"Yes, but the problem then is that they'll all want to come visit you."

"Well... then tell them I turned into a pigeon and flew away!"

Yaan caught Kel's other hand. "And why would you

do that?"

Kel's sunny smile lit his face. "I wouldn't." And he leaned in to kiss Yaan.

Now

Yaan's feet carried him straight to the Second Ward—where he proceeded to wander the streets, desperately hoping to stumble upon some sign of Kel. Without his last name, it had been impossible to look him up in the city directory. Now Yaan berated himself for never asking. Why hadn't he wanted to taste Kel's full name on his tongue? Why hadn't he considered the practical issue of one day needing to track Kel down with next to nothing to go on?

After another block of houses that all looked the same, any one of which Kel could've been inside for all he knew, the road spat him back out onto High Street. To the north, the walls of the Complex beckoned from their hill. Was it even worth going on? He was hungry, he'd abandoned his work, and his quest had been utterly fruitless so far...

When he glanced south, though, the sight of the brick orphans' home sitting stolidly on its corner conjured a map in his head. He turned his back on the Complex and strode further down until the building he sought came into view—the old Second theater.

His pace slowed as he took in the details. Masonry construction, three stories, stone cornice, coped roof. It was beautiful, of course; it had been designed to draw the eye, and consequently the crowds. He'd read the old treatise by the man who'd planned the city— "Edification through culture" had been his justification for putting a grand theater in the middle of a working-class neighborhood. A patronizing idea, but that wasn't why the theater had been closed...

On impulse, he stepped forward and reached out to touch the cool stone. Had the building really been so poorly constructed that it was already failing? Straightening his back and lifting his chin, as if he were off on government business, he stepped into the narrow alley skirting the building. The rotting smell from the stagnant puddles and piles of rubbish reminded him of home.

As he'd expected, the lock on the back door had been broken. Still, he hesitated before entering. What was he doing here? He wasn't going to find Kel in a decaying old building. But—Kel loved the place. And that was all

Yaan had right now.

In the dim corridor he pressed his sleeve to his nose against the mustiness; maybe the bad air would get him before the building's collapse could. Finally, stepping through an archway, he reached the foyer. Here the ceiling was a full two stories above him, and light filtered down from the edges of the boarded windows while the stone walls muffled the sounds of the street. It felt like another world.

He tipped his head back to study the tall columns supporting the ceiling; they had faces carved into the capitals, making all manner of expressions. When he turned he found the main doors before him, and he stepped forward to run his hand over the pattern of entwining vines and flowers carved into the dark wood. Beside it the wall's plaster had fallen away in places, revealing the stone underneath to be a lovely, pale blue strain of marble. Outside, the color had been grimed to gray.

An incongruity pulled his eyes downward. A hole gaped near the bottom of the wall, surrounded by jagged edges of plaster where an entire block of stone had been neatly removed. He crouched and frowned at it. Plaster dust lay like fresh snow on the floor.

This was too deliberate to be the work of common vandals. Yaan lifted his head to gaze up at the ceiling. There were no cracks there, nor any in the walls. No signs of structural instability at all. He rubbed some of the powder between his fingers, then rose and made for the back door.

III

Kel's family had been incredulous when he'd announced he was going to live with Yaan. "Why would you want to live there?" "How well do you even know him?" "Isn't he just another stuck-up official?"

"No, see, that's the thing," he answered the last. "He's not like the others; he doesn't care that I'm just a Second Ward delivery boy. He actually enjoys my company, and wants to know me. He... likes me." A blush crept over his cheeks. Acknowledging Yaan's interest aloud, not as a throwaway boast but as something he meant, and that meant something to him, made him self-conscious. Yaan could have been with anyone, and yet somehow, he had chosen Kel. That knowledge was a warm, ever-present glow inside his chest.

Now

Kel sat on the floor before the fire playing a post-dinner game of cards with Trayna and Beni, with Sarrin and Vari in chairs on either side. His mind was on the game, on how Trayna was winning for once, on the pleasant fullness of his stomach. Fixing on those things kept others from creeping in—until a knock sounded against the door.

Trayna looked toward the noise; Beni looked at Kel; Sarrin and Vari looked at each other. Kel's hand had frozen, still holding up the cards he'd been examining.

"I'll get it," Sarrin finally said, and ambled into the hall. Only her free arm remained in view as she opened the door.

"Hi. May I, uh, come in?"

The voice gave its owner away. "Is that him?" Trayna hissed at Kel, but he waved a hand to quiet her.

"I suppose," Sarrin grumbled, and a moment later she strode back into the room. Yaan stepped in after her.

Kel's face burned as he pictured the scene from

Yaan's perspective: him in his old, worn clothes, sitting on a long-faded rug, holding a bunch of battered playing cards. He dropped the latter and scrambled to his feet. As if Yaan had any respect for him to lose.

Yaan wasn't looking at his surroundings, though; his gaze was fixed on Kel. Stubble darkened his face, and his eyes had a wide, slightly wild look. Next to Kel, Trayna crawled to Beni's side. Kel caught her whisper: "He's *old.*" Beni immediately shushed her.

"Hi," Yaan finally said. Kel didn't answer; his speech wasn't working. "Can we talk?"

Vari rose from her seat, and Kel's head turned slowly toward her. "You don't have to, Kel. We can make him go if you want." She watched Kel, pointedly ignoring Yaan.

"Please—" Kel flapped his hand at her, willing her to sit and stop embarrassing him. "It's okay." She sighed and remained on her feet, but stayed quiet.

Kel turned back to Yaan, whose eyes were still on him. Wearing pants instead of a robe, a cloak hanging crooked from his shoulders, he didn't look at all like an official. The outer few layers of Kel's hurt sloughed away. He took a step forward.

"Yes," he said softly. He glanced back at Vari, his eyes

pleading with her not to argue. Her eyes told him he was making a mistake, but she didn't object otherwise.

Sarrin moved aside. Kel took another step. One of Yaan's hands lifted toward him, then dropped again. His expression had softened. "Do you want to take a walk?"

"Sure."

Kel followed Yaan to the door. Sarrin hovered behind them. "Take your coat." She pulled the garment off its peg and pressed it into Kel's hands.

"Thanks." He shrugged it on, then pulled open the door for Yaan. After a quick, self-conscious glance back, Yaan stepped out, and Kel threw Sarrin a closed-mouth smile before he followed.

They had all been so kind to him, mostly refraining from "we knew this would happen" sentiments, making sure he ate well, letting him sleep as long as he wanted that morning. He hoped they didn't feel betrayed.

"We're not selling the theater," Yaan blurted before they'd taken two steps away from the house. The gas lamp behind him left his face in shadow. "They wanted the stone—that particular variant has been quarried out, so it's a rare commodity now. They bribed the assessor to say the building was unstable so they could get the property cheap. They're all in legal trouble now, of course, and the sale's been canceled."

"Oh." Kel took a few steps in silence, letting the news settle. "How did you find out?"

"I went to the theater." Yaan cast him a sideways glance. "I came upon it when I was looking for you. They'd cut a piece of stone from the wall." After a moment, he added, "It really is beautiful."

"I'm glad it won't be destroyed." And he was, but his mind had snagged on a different part of Yaan's story. *I was looking for you.* He didn't know what he had expected when he'd left, but it hadn't been this—Yaan showing up at his home, having apparently searched the entire Second Ward.

"Look, Kel... I'm sorry." Yaan stopped under a lamp, face in full view now, and Kel stopped too, watching him. "About the meeting, about... everything. The commissioner came by and roped me into a long discussion, and I couldn't bring myself to send her away, but—I should have. I wish..." Yaan sucked in a long, unsteady breath. His eyes flitted to Kel's, then away again.

Kel stood, breathing the cool, slightly damp air. He should've known Yaan had a good reason. Or should he have? He opened his mouth to speak, but then closed it again, waiting for something more.

Then

"So, why the extra day?" Yaan had asked Peyan after they'd kissed hello. Peyan still tasted of dust from his travel.

"Genden's commissioner is interested in a personnel exchange." Peyan turned away, combing his hands through his hair in front of Yaan's mirror. "One of the personnel in question being me." Squinting at his reflection, he tamped down a stray lock. "I've decided to accept the offer."

"Oh." A vice clamped around Yaan's heart, formed of every fear about their relationship that had ever dogged him. That Peyan didn't like him as much as he liked Peyan. That Peyan would get bored with him. That Peyan would leave.

"So we'll both have to find someone new to keep us company." Peyan met Yaan's eyes in the mirror, flashing him a quick smile. "It's a shame, but I couldn't turn down the opportunity."

"Of course," Yaan agreed mechanically. He could

never ask Peyan to stay. How pitiable that would be, begging a man who probably wouldn't even miss him, who was probably looking forward to finding someone new. At least Yaan could maintain his dignity, and never let Peyan know how deeply his choice had cut.

Now

Yaan swallowed and dragged his eyes up to Kel's face again. Kel was still looking at him, an unreadable mask in place of his usual expressiveness. "Kel." Yaan's voice broke on the word. His hand reached out, fingers brushing Kel's before withdrawing again. Kel didn't reciprocate, but he didn't flinch away, either.

Yaan hadn't stopped to rest or eat all day. After sorting out the theater mess, he'd scoured the most recent census for any 19-year-old resident of the Second Ward who might be nicknamed "Kel" and lived with two parents and a plethora of siblings. Kellian Insporo, son of Sarrin and Vari, had fit, and the directory had done the rest.

Now, with his well of words nearly dry, he dredged up everything he had left. "You make me happy." His tone was pathetic, pleading, but he pressed on. "Just being around you. You're so cheerful, and kind, and curious, and I'm lucky to get to be a part of your life. I know I lost sight of that for a bit. I've been so preoccupied with myself, I..." His fists clenched and unclenched at his sides. "I stopped seeing you. I stopped thinking about what you needed, or wanted. You had every right to feel the way you did."

Kel wore an almost dazed expression, but still didn't speak. Yaan stared at him for a long moment before blurting, "Can I kiss you?" He took one, small step closer, then paused, holding his breath.

Kel was still for countless heartbeats, dark eyes gazing questioningly back. Then, very slightly, he nodded.

Yaan stepped forward to bring them chest-to-chest. The familiar position, one he'd never thought anything of before, sent spikes of terror through him. If he fucked this up, again, one or both of them was going to shatter into pieces. His run-and-hide instincts were almost as strong as on annual-review day.

But—this was Kel. Who, against all logic, was giving him another chance. How could he not take it?

His hands were shaking slightly, but he pressed them to Kel's cheeks anyway. Kel looked back at him, and Yaan ached to know what he was thinking. Echoes of the ways he'd tried to placate Kel in the past rang in his mind—spouted excuses, easy lies, whatever came into his head. Look where that had gotten him.

Leaning in, he let his lips brush over Kel's, and Kel's breath drew in with a catch. Yaan gently took Kel's bottom lip in both of his. Kel's eyes fluttered shut, and Yaan closed his, too, and kissed Kel with all the tenderness and affection he'd held inside for so long. "I adore you," he whispered, drawing back just enough to say the words before kissing Kel again. "I want to make you as happy as you make me." Another kiss. "I'm so sorry I ever made you doubt that."

Kel's hands settled on his waist, and when he kissed Yaan back, the dam in Yaan's chest burst. When they drew apart, Kel's face was beautifully flushed, eyes glistening in the light. For a moment they just stared at each other. Then Kel sniffed, blinking rapidly a few times as his face broke into a smile. "You mean it." He wrapped his arms around Yaan, laying his head on Yaan's shoulder and nuzzling his face into Yaan's neck. Yaan clasped him tightly in return, trying and failing to stave off a visit from his own tears.

❧

Kel walked into the outer office and tossed a smile at Ori, who raised his eyebrows in return. After a tap on Yaan's door, and the muffled "Yes?", he stepped inside.

"Got a message for you." He pinched his mouth into an even line.

"Oh?" Yaan's deadpan was far superior. "Let's have it, then."

"All right. The message is... it's time to stop working and come with me!" Kel flung out his arms and spun in a circle, meaning to step around Yaan's desk as he did so but instead bumping into it. Yaan scrambled up, and Kel gave him a sheepish look before stepping into his arms for a kiss.

Drawing back, Kel slipped his hand into Yaan's and tugged him toward the door, but Yaan kept his feet planted. "Wait, wait, let me just straighten up here..."

Kel let go, side-eyeing the few ledgers and papers on the desk. Yaan stood over them, hesitating, then said, "You know what, it's fine. I'll deal with it tomorrow. Just let me get the key..."

As they left the room, it was Yaan who took Kel's hand, and continued to hold it as they bid good night to Ori and made their way through the halls. Kel had an urge to pull away, to fall back to walk a step behind Yaan. A messenger boy in dusty, scuffed boots wasn't meant to be hand-in-hand with a robed official. But Yaan never faltered.

"Are you still okay with going to my family's afterward?" Kel asked when they'd gotten through the gates, out into the sunlight and openness of the street. "Because we don't have to, I can let them know today's not good after all." The terror that had darted across Yaan's face when Kel had made the suggestion still played in his mind, even though Yaan had assented immediately afterward.

Yaan squeezed his hand. "I'm not about to back out now." A smile took over Kel's face.

Upon reaching the Second theater, they stopped to gaze up at its facade. "It's a good building," Yaan said. "Someday it'll be alive again."

Kel leaned into him for a moment in reply, then asked, "Ready?"

"After you." Yaan loosed his fingers from Kel's to draw the key from his pocket and hold it out. With a grin, Kel took it and stepped up to the door, Yaan close by his side. As one of his hands found Yaan's again, the other slid the key into the lock.

ACKNOWLEDGMENTS

First, thank you to my two early readers of this story, Rosa and Zan—your feedback helped me shape *Structural Integrity* into its final form, and I am so very appreciative.

Thank you to all the self-pub veterans who answered my newbie questions and helped me see that the process wasn't so scary after all.

Thank you to my lovely writing friends for all the support, both pre- and post-publication! (And an extra thank you to those who helped me through my self-taught crash course in paperback formatting.)

Finally, thank you to the wonderful people who asked about and encouraged the creation of physical copies of my little novellas. *Structural Integrity* exists in physical form now because of you. <3

SEQUEL PREVIEW

STRUCTURAL STRAIN

After realizing how badly he was failing his partner, Yaan promised to do better. Being open and vulnerable with Kel isn't exactly easy, but it's worth it for the closeness they now share. Kel, meanwhile, continues to combat his conflict-avoidant nature and be honest about his own wants and needs. The payoff includes not just an increase in affection from Yaan, but also Yaan getting to know his family, and even pledging to help get the old neighborhood theater—the catalyst for their reconciliation—open again.

When Yaan begins noticing other ways the city government he works for has failed its working-class residents, his renewed commitment to Kel leads him to push back against his boss's policies. Kel, however, is concerned Yaan might be taking on too much. When he's proven right, their relationship will be tested anew, as Yaan is forced to decide what really matters to him and Kel must choose how far he's willing to go for Yaan's sake.

Dread twisted in Yaan's stomach as Kel burst into his family's house without knocking, calling out, "We're here!" He hesitated on the threshold while Kel pulled off his coat; it would be so easy to take a step backward and escape... But then Kel glanced over his shoulder, offering an encouraging smile when their eyes met. "Hey, come on in." He stretched out his hand, and Yaan swallowed, stepped forward, and took it.

One of Kel's sisters was emerging from the kitchen, the older one—Beni. She wore a stained apron, hair pulled back into a braid with several wisps snaking free. It was strange seeing Kel's eyes in her face.

"Hi." She grinned at Kel, smile softening but still lingering when she looked at Yaan. "Welcome. We're all just in here, finishing up..."

"Tell them to wait out there," a voice hissed from behind her.

Beni's face tinged pink. "Um, well, I guess—"

A shriek from the kitchen cut her off; it was quickly muffled, followed by a buzz of heated whispers.

"I should—" Beni grimaced at Kel, gave a helpless shrug, and disappeared back through the doorway.

Yaan's free hand stilled on his coat buttons. "I'm ruining their night, I can go…"

Kel rolled his eyes, his grip staying firm. "It's not ruined, and if it was it'd be their own fault. Come on."

"But they said—"

"Ridiculous." Kel shook his head as he pulled Yaan along. "Treating me like a guest in my own home." He raised his voice on the second sentence, making Yaan cringe.

"No, Kel, wait—" Sarrin appeared in the kitchen doorway, blocking their way with a hand pressed to either side of the frame. "We're not *ready*."

"That's fine." Kel rose onto his toes to kiss her on the cheek. "We'll help."

Her eyes slid to Yaan. He tried to smile, but was certain it looked rather grisly. "Yes, right, I'd be happy to—help." Even though he'd never cooked a speck of food in his life.

"Ugh, just let them in!" A young voice—Trayna.

"Hey—" Sarrin twisted her head around, and Kel took the chance to slip under her arm. "Hey!" She shook her head and glanced at Yaan again, and gods she was just as intimidating as the commissioner and his instinct was certainly to back away and take a seat in the main room and wait there quiet and still until his presence was called for, but before he could she sighed and dropped her arms. "Well, come on in then. Sorry for the mess, and the lateness... everything would have been ready and waiting for you if *someone* hadn't burned the first batch of sauce."

"You told me it didn't need constant stirring!" Trayna exclaimed.

"Hey..." Kel was an island of calm in the middle of the room. "It's fine. We don't mind."

And it was true. It would have been much worse if they'd all been sitting silently at the table, waiting for him and Kel.

Beni stood at the stove, stirring a pot that was likely the source of the sharp, lemony scent in the air. Vari was brushing crumbs from the table as Sarrin set a large, towel-covered dish on it. Trayna clutched a handful of utensils with one hand and pawed through a drawer with the other.

Something about the scene pricked at Yaan. An old memory stirred in his mind: stumbling home from the warehouse his parents managed, eyes bleary from reading manifests and scribbling in ledgers all day, into the kitchen where there might be a pot of boiled meat and potatoes kept warm on the hearth. He'd serve himself a bowl and eat alone in silence, or if no meal awaited him, scrounge a half-eaten tin of stale biscuits from the cupboard. One of his parents would be asleep already, the other still out dealing with last-minute business. Half the time he'd trudge off to bed in the dark, not bothering to light a candle.

"You're a sweetheart, Kel." Vari straightened, briskly brushing off her hands, and fluffed his hair. It matched hers, dark and straight, contrasting with Sarrin's curls.

"Hi." Kel beamed at her, and then—to Yaan's horror—met Yaan's eyes, and beckoned him over.

Structural Strain *is available now in ebook and paperback!*

ABOUT THE AUTHOR

Tabitha O'Connell is a historic preservationist and writer of queer fiction living in Western New York. Eir favorite things include animals, abandoned places, alliteration, long walks, and long sentences (some of which may or may not turn up in eir work...). Right now ey is probably drinking tea and daydreaming about stories centering ace, trans, and other queer characters.

Keep up with em via...

- Website: tabithaoconnell.com
- Twitter: @tabithawrites
- Instagram: @tabitha.writes
- Newsletter: tabithaoconnell.com/newsletter

9 798201 032999